Inside

John and Marilyn Talbot

Illustrated by Rhiannon Powell

Contents

Red Card

'It's a red card and Valentine is sent off!
Steve Valentine is going off the pitch!
What a blow to United.'

Tony and Ben could hardly bear to look.
United were two up at half time, but now,
in extra time, they were 3:2 down!

It was all over and United were out of the Cup!
'If Steve Valentine hadn't been sent off, this
would never have happened,' said Tony.
'It's all his fault,' said Ben.

Everyone felt the same way.
Steve Valentine had let them all down.
'VALENTINE MUST GO!'
said the newspapers.

Day and night the Press camped outside his
door waiting for him to come out.
'What have you got to say for yourself?'
they asked.
But Steve Valentine said nothing.

'I have to get away from all this,' Steve Valentine said to his wife. 'Take the car and wait for me around the corner.'

Then he went out by the back door,
jumped over the fence and ran over to the car.
His wife walked back to the house
and Steve Valentine drove off into the night.

'BAD BOY STEVE VALENTINE ON THE RUN,'
said the newspapers.
The Press and TV looked for him everywhere.
They even put up a reward of £1,000 for him.

Steve Valentine had gone to stay with his aunt in Wellington Square.
From her window he looked out at people in the street and he felt trapped.
'Your tea's getting cold,' said Mrs Valentine, but Steve wasn't listening.

That night Steve Valentine put on a hat
and went out for a walk in the Square.
He had started to grow a beard to hide his face.
As he walked he kept his head down.
He didn't look at anyone or anything.

If he had looked in the window of number
19 Wellington Square he would have seen
Tessa Potts working on her old computer,
but he didn't.

Tessa was the editor of the school magazine.
The next magazine was coming out soon
and she needed just one more story.

Chapter 2

The Stranger

One night, after school, Tony and Ben were kicking a ball about in Wellington Square.

Tony was in goal. Ben kicked the ball into the road and it landed at Steve Valentine's feet. Steve Valentine kicked it back across the street, past Tony and into the goal!

'Did you see that!' yelled Tony.

'That was cool,' said Ben.

'That was sooooo cool,' they said.

'Hey, Mister, come back!' shouted Tony.

'Show us how you did that!'

But the man just ran off around the corner.

That night Tony told everyone what
the stranger did.
'Who was he?' Tessa asked.
'Don't know, he was a stranger,' said Tony.
'But what did he look like?' she asked.
'Well, he was tall with a beard,' said Tony.

A few days later Tessa was in Wellington
Square when she saw the stranger.
He looked away but Tessa was sure she had
seen him before.

Back home she saw her dad's newspaper
with a picture of the missing footballer.
Tessa got a pen and drew a beard
on the face.

'It's him, the stranger is Steve Valentine,'
thought Tessa.
'Mrs Valentine said she was the aunt of a
famous footballer, but we didn't think it
was true!'

Tessa went out into the Square.
She waited for Steve Valentine to come back.
She didn't have to wait long.
As he walked past she called out, 'Steve?'
He turned, but didn't stop. Tessa ran after him.
'It's you, isn't it, Steve Valentine?'
He was just about to go inside.
'It's OK, I won't give you away, I don't want
the reward,' she said.

'What do you want?' he asked.

'An interview,' she said.

'Why should I give you an interview?
All newspapers do is print lies!' he said.

'I'm not from the newspapers,' said Tessa.

'Who are you then?' he asked.

'I'm from the school magazine and I promise not to print lies,' said Tessa.
She gave Steve Valentine a note with her name and mobile phone number.
'Even if you don't give me an interview, I still won't tell where you are,' she said.
Steve Valentine took the note, went inside and closed the door.

Tessa went home. The news was on TV.
'Where is Steve Valentine?' said the reporter.
'He has gone into hiding. He hasn't been seen
for two weeks now.'
Tessa wanted to shout out, 'I know where he is!'
But she didn't say a word to anyone.

Chapter 3

The Interview

A few days later Tessa got a phone call from
Steve Valentine.

'OK, you kept your word,' he said. 'Come over
and I will give you an interview for your
school magazine.'

Tessa was amazed, a real interview with
Steve Valentine. Wow!

Mrs Valentine had made them a pot of tea and some cakes.

'Ask me anything you like,' said Steve.

'Do you like your job as a footballer?' asked Tessa.

'Yes, I love it, it's what I do best.
But sometimes it gets too much for me.
People want me to win all the time
and that's hard, very hard.'

'What are you hiding from?' asked Tessa.
Steve Valentine looked hard at her and Tessa
thought he was going to get cross, but he didn't.
'I'm hiding from everyone,' he said, 'from
people who hate me for doing one bad thing.
I let myself down, but more than that, I let my
fans down. I can't face up to what I did.'

21

Over the next day Tessa worked on the story
at her old computer.
As soon as the school magazine was printed
she put a copy in Mrs Valentine's letter box.

It didn't take long
before the newspapers
found out about the school magazine.
Who was this girl who had got the inside story?

Soon the Press were outside the school
and it was Tessa they wanted to see.
It was her turn to be interviewed.
Now she knew how Steve Valentine felt.

'Yes, I do know where Steve Valentine is,' said Tessa, 'but I won't tell you because he asked me not to. Steve gave me the interview because I said I would print the truth. Well I did, and you can read it in our school magazine. That's all I've got to say.'

Chapter 4

Found Out

Tony and Ben had also seen the school magazine. And it didn't take them long to put two and two together.

'I bet I know who the stranger is,' said Tony.

'I bet I know where he is,' said Ben.

The boys ran over to Mrs Valentine's house
and rang the bell.
Mrs Valentine opened the door.
'Is Steve in?' they asked.
'Just a moment,' she said and the boys could
hear her talking to someone.
'Tell them to come in,' a voice said.

'So Tessa told you I was here,' he said.
'No, she didn't, we just worked it out,' said Ben.
'You kicked our ball, it was so cool,' said Tony.
Steve Valentine laughed.
'So that's what gave me away, a rash kick.
That's the story of my life. Well, now you get
the reward,' said Steve.

'We don't want the reward,' said Tony.
'So what do you want?' asked Steve.
'Just to play a game of football with you,'
they said.
Steve Valentine hadn't played for two weeks
and it was the thing he most wanted to do in
all the world.
'Alright,' he said 'but there are a few things
I've got to do first.'

Steve Valentine had made up his mind he wasn't going to hide any more – not from the Press, not from the TV, not from himself.
But first he had to call someone on his mobile.

'Tessa, you can tell the Press where I am now. You deserve the reward,' he said. 'And Tessa, thank you for being such a good reporter.'

Then he shaved off his beard.

When the Press arrived in Wellington Square,
they saw Steve Valentine playing football
with Tony and Ben.
They took a lot of pictures.
But Steve didn't stop to talk to them,
he just smiled and went on playing.
He didn't have anything more to say.
'It's all in the school magazine,' he yelled.

The next day the newspapers were full of it. There were lots of pictures of Tessa, and pictures of the boys playing football with Steve Valentine.

Soon Steve Valentine was back playing football for United.

Tessa smiled when she saw him on TV.
But she was already working on the next magazine with the new laptop she bought with the reward money.

Tony and Ben also watched the game on TV. It was great to see Steve Valentine playing again, and to see him score the winning goal for United.

'Steve Valentine is cool,' said Tony.

'Sooooo cool,' said Ben.